THE YELLOW CAFÉ COLLECTION

A book of verse

By

Graham Gladstone

ABOUT THE AUTHOR

Graham Gladstone is a both a regular visitor and regular contributor at the celebrated arts venue The Yellow Café. He was born in Liverpool many years after the musical and poetical surge of the city during the 1960s and yet it was his local poet, Adrian Henri, born in Birkenhead, who inspired him to write what was known as 'The Liverpool Scene' poetry.

It was whilst visiting Henri's grave in Montparnesse Cemetry in Paris when he met with Lana, The Yellow Café waitress. She told him The Yellow Café were in search of a resident poet, and so it was the Graham joined the team of freedom and liberation.

Not just his works, but his recitals are an important feature of the café and his popularity there has expanded his awareness to schools and colleges throughout the local area, both reciting and teaching modern poetry.

This is his one and only collection of verse and he dedicates the book to all those he works alongside at such an amazing venue.

The Yellow Café

Its doors are as open as your mind allows
Creaking doors grown old
Doors that hid away for many years
Tales of yesteryear untold
Once upon a time where I sit now
Grain and wheat stacked high
Harvested by weary farmers
As the winter months drew nigh
Time moves on
Such men have long gone
Machinery has turned into song

Only a matter of a few years ago
Those doors were opened wide
To reveal a barn of imagination
That passages of time could not hide
The machinery went to the scrapyard
Its operators to the graveyard
All was as still as the night within
Secrets that were held within
Time moves on
The barn was built too strong
To fall like those who have gone

The smell of oil would have filled their nostrils
Dust would block the chest
That was the way until it closed
Probably for the best

It's now the smell of coffee
That glides from beam to beam
It's now the sound of music
Not an overworked machine
Time moves on
The machinery has gone
Replaced by poetry and song

The fields around they haven't changed
They have no reason why they should
Oh no these fields will never change
Even if they could
These fields were here long before us all
Ignoring changing times
As green as they were a century back
Their stubbornness brightly shines
Time moves on
Their lifetime has been long
And will continue when we've gone

They exchanged stories just like us
Broke bread to break their toil
Bales of hay where chairs are now placed
Weary workers of the soil
String tying up their shirt-sleeves
Boots as strong as heavy horses
Perhaps mead to wash down their luncheon
Just one but not three courses
Time moves on
For that tired yet wear throng

Things would change they knew that all along

To escape from the world I come here
I sit where those men sit
The walls and windows haven't changed
Or maybe a little bit
The old barn experienced decay
It knew its time was up
Kind of sleeping with nothing much to say
As it watched the final sup
Time moves on
With fortune the barn got it wrong
Now it's a place of art and song

Its doors are as open as mind allows
Creaking doors grown old
Doors that hid away for many years
Tales of yesteryear untold
Once upon a time where I sit now
Grain and wheat stacked high
Harvested by weary farmers
As the winter months drew nigh
Time moves on
Such men have long gone
Machinery has turned into song
I feel the barn knew that all along

Elephants

They were here before the cave-man's birth
They were here before us on the Earth
We made them walk round circus rings
Made them do ridiculous things
We treated the creature so unkind
They forgave us all I think we'll find
As we left them like unwanted pets
But remember an elephant never forgets

At times of war they carried our soldiers
On their broad endangered shoulders
They have always been there by our side
For moving logs or having a ride
We took things Mother Nature planted
We took elephant's rights for granted
We took the waters where they drink
We took the elephants to the brink

So now our gratitude we must show
To help them out before they go
We must help the elephant to survive
We must help the elephant stay alive
Now the pay-back time has come
We must help them every single one
For the loyalty they have given man
We must help them get through if we can

As the world gets ever stranger
Remember the elephant is in danger
All we can say is 'sorry mate'
And help them before it gets too late
Remember how badly we've behaved
Remember the elephant must be saved
Remember they are nature's greatest gem
They need us now like we needed them

Darkened Room

Sitting in my darkened room
Waiting patiently for the Moon
To come out of hiding behind a cloud
To light the sky to sit there proud
The Moon sometimes makes me smile
When I'm feeling down a while
Then when the Moon away shall creep
I close my eyes and go to sleep

Sitting in my lightened room
It's now not night but afternoon
I shall not see the Moon a while
So for a while I shall not smile
But the Moon comes out tonight
I know I'm going to feel alright
Even if it pours with rain
I know I'll go to sleep again

This poem may not be alright
But it is the first one I have tried to write
If the Moon gives light tonight
My second one I'll try and write

The White Caravan at The Yellow Cafe

He is someone in my head who won't go away
He is someone in my head who seems to want to stay
So now is the time to tell you if I can
Of Charlie and his white caravan
Charlie had white hair, Charlie wore a white coat
Charlie was as welcome as a white wooden lifeboat
And that's how the memory began
Of Charlie and his white caravan

Cockles and mussels, prawns in brine
Outside the pub at closing time
Winkles whelks, shrimps in a cup
Outside the pub when time was up
It's a memory of a very special man
Charlie and his white caravan
Charlie and his white caravan

Charlie's caravan was not beside the sea
Or high upon a cliff-top where others tend to be
You'd never ever find beside the sand
Charlie and his white caravan
No it wasn't by the seaside but yes it should have been there
By the water's edge it was sadly never seen there
But picture the fragrance if you can
Of Charlie and his white caravan

Cockles and mussels, prawns in brine
Outside the pub at closing time
Winkles whelks, shrimps in a cup
Outside the pub when time was up
It's a memory of a very special man

Charlie and his white caravan
Charlie and his white caravan

That's why the old man means so much to me
the nearest I ever came to swimming in the sea
So now you understand
Charlie and his white caravan
Charlie was my beach, Charlie was my free ride
Charlie was the closest that I ventured to the seaside
That's why it was high time that I sang
Of Charlie and his white caravan

Happy Birthday To Me

It's my birthday today and I'm a long way from home
So I'm having a party all on my own
Happy birthday to me happy birthday to me
Happy birthday dear Graham

Happy birthday to me
You may think I'm incredibly sad
But I don't give a jot what a great day I've had
Thank you Yellow Café for being my friend
From me to you this poem I send

Close Your Eyes

Please don't hurt your arms
You cannot move a mountain
Don't talk seal your lips
You can't drink dry a fountain
Close your eyes
Go home as the crow flies
That's the shortest distance
To your lover's arms

Please don't let me die
Said the man upon the gallows
Let me rest in peace
Said the old fish in the shallows
The man is no more
The fish is safe close to the shore
So close your eyes
Let what happens be

If you break my heart
Please don't throw away the pieces
For I will mend it some day
When my new love increases
Not needle and thread
But happiness and smiles instead
And I will go my way
And I will close my eyes

The Pink Dolphin

A school of dolphins swimming by
Glinting eyes
Gentle smiles
Swimming together
I see them pass
A school of dolphins
An entire class
One is missing
Late for school
In fact she didn't turn up at all
She didn't have the uniform
Because she was pink when she was born

Boys In The Bath

Boys in the bath having a laugh
Bright red arms and bright red faces
Ducks splashing sponges crashing
So Fabulous this place is
Giggling wriggling end of a day
Washing all the sunburn away
Sleepy heads time for their beds
Dreaming of more sun next day
Time to own up time for the grown ups
Putting a few wines away
Watching the sunset breathing a sigh
Young eyes missing midnight kissing
Make sure they're asleep into bedroom creep
Dreaming away time to play
But no glorious noise
Mustn't wake up the boys

The Guitar Player

Hokus Pokus
How I loved Focus
Guitar strings bending
High notes descending

Time to play
So buy a guitar
Learning and learning
Not getting too far

Hard skin on fingers
Neighbours hate me so much
The guitar is to watch
But never to touch

Eric Clapton must have started like me
Jimi Hendrix too
Jan Akkerman was born a genius
And so Jan this poem's for you

Joggers

Have you ever seen jogger guys trying to run
Hell! They don't seem to have too much fun
They wear those headbands that make them sweat
And Swatches the size of a jumbo jet

Monumental trainers the size of trays
And ragged shorts that have seen better days
Have you ever seen jogger guys trying to run
Hey, I've just realised you guys, I am one

Blue to Red

How many colours
Turn a sunset into night?
How many colours more
To bring the morning light?
A paintbox of magic hues
So many in the sky to choose
From purple reds to midnight blues
Many many hundreds

Make up this magical chart
When clouds become paintbrushes
Allowing the change to start
Brushing softly across the sky
That's what rainclouds do
Painting colours adding tints
To change from red to blue
Then blue turns to black

As the rainclouds go to sleep
And then from blue to red next day
As the rainclouds start to weep
How many colours
Turn a sunset into night?
How many colours more
To bring the morning light?

Do You Have Dreams?

Do you have dreams?
Do they come true?
Because I'm not all that sure they do
I long to hear my mobile phone
I've almost forgotten its ringing tone
If dreams come true the phone would ring
But tonight I can't hear anything

Do you have dreams?
Do dreams come true?
Ring my phone and prove to me they do

More Than Anything Else

More than anything else I want be free
More than anything else I want to be me
More than anything else I want be free
More than anything else taken seriously

More than anything else I want to be free
More than anything else I so want to be
More than anything else someone with caring
More than anything else I want to be sharing

More than anything else the beauty of life
More than anything else to eliminate strife
More than anything else I want to be free
More than anything else I want you to agree

I Met a Lady

We met I guess in the worst of places
And the question was "Who held all the aces?"

I saw you dressed in colours pale
While others dressed to catch a male
Your suit did not your figure flatter
Just a small point which does not matter
A girl's not judged on what she wears
Its other things that get men's stares
Like figures legs long hair and faces
Yes Girls you see hold all the aces
We met now you have forgotten me
But I am left with your memory
A soft voice and a gorgeous face
That's framed with hair that's soft as lace

So blonde you are will always be
The wife I wish was meant for me

I Almost Did

I almost said
You might have responded

I almost asked
You might have replied

I almost did
You might have reacted

I saw you leave
I almost followed

I wonder now
What might have happened

If I'd done
What I almost did

Mr Prostate

I was honoured to have been asked to write this poem
by the local Rotary Club when they visited The Yellow
Café for a fund-raising lunch.

The Rotary wheels are turning round
The Rotary wheels are making ground
Yes our goal may take a while
But we'll get nearer every mile
So until the answer can be found
The Rotary Wheels are turning round

On your bike Mr Prostate
We don't want you round here
On your bike Mr Prostate
It's time to disappear
We'll cycle if you dip into your pocket or your purse
Cos Mr Prostate you're a pain and you're a curse

The Rotary wheels are turning round
The Rotary wheels are making ground
Yes our goal may take a while
But we'll get nearer every mile
So until the answer can be found
The Rotary Wheels are turning round

On your bike Mr Prostate
You're a pain in the proverbial rear
On your bike Mr Prostate
Give us the all-clear
Yes we'll get on our bikes if you get on yours too

And we'll be so delighted to see the back of you

The Rotary wheels are turning round
The Rotary wheels are making ground
Yes our goal may take a while
But we'll get nearer every mile
So until the answer can be found
The Rotary Wheels are turning round

A Very Special Ring

Would you find it funny if this song is not?
Would you find it funny if the funnies I forgot?
Funnies make you laugh and that's my usual style
Here's a song that isn't but I hope it makes you smile

Having said all that, it's funny we both know
How our eyes both met so many years ago
We went our different ways and here's the funny thing
We somehow stayed together through a very special
ring

Sixteen years of wondering but I didn't know what for
Bottles of tequila that crashed me to the floor
Sixteen years of moving on with other girls instead
Sixteen years not knowing you were always in my head

It's funny but it isn't how I won your heart
Sixteen years together when sixteen years apart
You went your way I went mine but here's the funny
thing
We always stayed together through a very special ring

Would you find it funny if I have my say?
If I'm being funny in a funny sort of way
Would you find it funny if I laugh every day?
When I think about the special ring you never threw
away

Sixteen years of wondering but I didn't know what for
Bottles of tequila that crashed me to the floor
Sixteen years of moving on with other girls instead
Sixteen years not knowing you were always in my head

Someone Special

I know I'm not an extrovert
Or say what's on my mind
I'm really just an introvert
Whose eyes are never blind

My eyes beheld your wondrous grace
Exquisite beauty too!
This beauty shines out from your face
And every pore of you

But what is you is still not seen
Despite how hard one looks
By talking some is shown I mean
By that's not learnt in books

I'd like to talk to get to know
The you I see before
For outer beauty's only show
The inner counts lots more

You may now think that I'm a child
Despite my many years
I'm honest loving tender mild
With adult hopes and fears

When Do I Love Thee?

When do I love thee? Let me count the times!
(I tried to write a verse to this, but it just never rhymes.)

When I awake I think of you
and see the sun arise
My heart begins to see you there
Yes my most precious prize

The warming rays the sun pours forth
Are like your loving rays
The sun's warmth lands on everyone
Your love just cheers my days

When morning ends and noon has come
And all's still going right
I look around to see you there
Your face that smiles so bright

When work does end I think of you
Just as your day begins
I'm wishing I could share with you
My losses and my wins

When my day ends I dream of you
And see you there with me
Laughing, loving, smiling, crying
You're there - eternally

But if a day should bring the rain
It still won't make me sad
I know it's just your loss I'll feel
Shared thoughts will make me glad!

And when I stop to pray to GOD
You're always in my prayers
Your safety is most paramount
Plus solace from your cares.

Yes! Darling, I still think of you
As through the day I go
And knowing that you think of me
Ensures I have no woe

Your Best Friend

Wherever you are hiding
Wherever you may sneak
Wherever you are hiding
I shall come and seek
If ever you are missing
If you are not around
I promise I will find you
In the lost and found

Wherever you are running
And whoever you run from
Wherever you are running
You shall never run too long
If ever you're escaping
From something you detest
I shall come and find you

I shall do my very best
Whenever you are pleading
For mercy on your knees
When your heart is bleeding
I shall hear those pleas
Whatever has been done
I promise I shall mend
Whatever happens I'll be there
Because I'm your best friend

If I Was Given One More Day

If I was given one more day
If I was given one more word to say
If I was given one more chance
If I was given one last dance

If I was given one more text
If I was given the next and the next
If I was given one email
To win your heart I wouldn't fail

If I was given one more day
If I could rub out yesterday
If I was given today instead
If was given right words to be said

If I was given you back again
I know I wouldn't act the same
I'm not really humpy or over-sexed
All I want is one short text!!

On The Level

On the level
I don't know what I did
On the level
I think I simply slid

On the level
I never ever knew it
But on the level
It seems I went and blew it

On the level
Will you take me back?
On the level
I hate being on my Jack

On the level
Let's go one more time around
On the level
This time I won't let you down

Dinner At The Yellow Cafe

Tonight I'm dining out alone
There's only me and my mobile phone
Someone might ring out of the blue
And then I'll be having a dinner for two

I'm still on my own and I'm not surprised
My phones on silent and I never realised
So here I sit with sweet and sour balls
A bowl of rice and three missed calls

Just Remember We're Here

During your darkness in hours of need
I hope these words you will heed

Count your blessings say your prayers
We are watching but we do not stare

Look to loved ones hold those thoughts
Fight the fight it can be fought

Should your mind wander should you despair
Remember you're loved and that we care

Shadows will lift and light will show
You'll be fine and on you will go

So look forward bravely you've a lot to embrace
And if you can put a smile on your face

Remember that laughter is good for you
We can laugh too we'll see this thing through

During your darkness in hours of need
I hope these words you will heed

Reformed Gambler

Years ago I did the pools
Bet on horses stood in the stalls
Bet on flies climbing up walls
Bet I couldn't cross Niagara Falls

Years ago I played roulette
17 red I placed a bet
Did I win? I forget
Bet I'd swim the Channel without getting wet

Years ago I bet on the dogs
Bet on the height of jumping frogs
Bet on how long people would spend in the bogs
It was all as easy as falling off logs

Years ago I bet a million
That in five years I'd be worth a billion
I invented a tandem that had no pillion
I lost the bet but married Gillian

We All Make Mistakes

There is room for human error
It happens to us all
Accepting such a weakness
Helps us to stand tall

We all make mistakes
For as long as we all live
Yet sometimes the hardest thing of all
Is to cuddle and forgive

Give Me The Time

Give me the time
To make something of myself
Give me the time
Give me the health
Give me the time
To play my part
Give me the time
Give me the heart

Show me the sign
That leads me to win
Show me the sign
Of how I begin
Show me the sign
To be a man
Show me the sign
And I'll do what I can

Love

Where does love come from? How do we find
Is it in body or is it in mind
Then there is passion for some that is all
But how do we know which is which when we fall

Time will take over and help us to find
Which was in body or was it in mind
For true love is there and you know it is real
You have to admit you know how you feel

So onward together for certain we will
Find happiness together
For love is a sure and means everything
So enjoy what we have whenever we can
For who knows how much time we have left
for each other

The Star That Shines So Bright

You are the star of the night
The one up there that shines so bright
I think of loss as I sit on the moss
By your grave I try to be brave
But it's hard to hide the feelings inside

As I sit and try not to cry
I know you're always in my heart
So we will never part
So all I can do is sit with you
As there's nothing else left for me to do

Please Don't Forget

You can forget birthdays as much as you like
You can forget Christmas cards too
All I ask is don't forget me
And I promise I won't forget you

Please don't forget last night
The time we spent together
You can forget Easter Eggs and stuff like that
But please remember last night forever

Don't Give Me A Reason

Don't give me a reason to say goodbye
Don't give me a reason to make you cry
Don't give me a reason to walk away
Give me a reason as to why I should stay

Don't give me a reason to doubt you at all
To wonder why you did not make that call
Don't give a reason to think the worst
Don't let me think our bubble has burst

Don't give me a reason to think you're too busy
Don't say he's more important than me. Is he?
This rhyme is pleading that this isn't true
Turning blind eyes on what I already knew

Don't give me a reason no reason is needed
You can't make me cry I've already conceded
You can't give me a reason to walk away
You already have, you went yesterday

I Need You

I need help
I need fortitude
Togetherness
And solitude
A fortress where no-one can enter
A safe-house where nobody can leave
Can I find my saviour to bring both to my soul?

Maybe it is you
That can help to get me through
With things and deeds you do
Yes my saviour could well be you
I don't need to know you
To make me strong
You are my spirit

To repair me that is wrong
A mender of meanings
A purveyor of proof
A lover of love
And a teller of truth
That's why I need you

Don't Do That To Me Again

I can take it once
But I can't take it twice
Once is ok
Twice is not very nice
Three times
I will crack
Three times
And I'm never coming back
So before you treat me bad again
Before you dish me out more pain
Before you expect me to remain
Don't do that to me again

Once is just an accident
Twice is rather cruel
Three times means the point is made
And you've broken every rule
Once is enough
Once is making me feel rough
Twice will be a mistake
Because two times I cannot take
Three times is ridiculous
Even though I'm meek
Three Chinese take-aways
Is too much in one week

English Floods

A little down the road from here
The sea is coming in
A little down the road from here
Folk are drenched through to the skin
England is under water
Tempers are getting shorter
They have no drinking water

A little down the road from here two rivers have
collided
A little down the road from here two bridges have
subsided
Surely this can't be global warming?
They can't say they weren't given warning
It's enough to just make a visit
That isn't the real solution is it?
Build us higher walls and a deeper drain
Make sure the floods don't come again

A little down the road from here
The sea is coming in
A little down the road from here
Folk are drenched through to the skin
England is under water
Tempers are getting shorter
They have no drinking water

Damn the Drizzle

Damn the drizzle and damn the rain
Will we ever see the Sun shine again?
Something's going on up there
Something's happening in the air
Politicians still are stalling
But the rain it just keeps on a-falling
Summers now are much much shorter
English cities are out of water
All those countries who we gave aid
Where are they now? Nowhere I'm afraid
Water water everywhere and not a drop to drink
It used to be a song but now it's more I think
Who'd ever thought it possible?
In our green and pleasant land?
Climate change is here
The green fields disappear
Beauty spots sinking now
They don't know why and they don't know how
Summer days are now history
Nothing like they used to be
Sunny days out of reach
No more days as kids on the beach
Water water everywhere
It may not be right and it may not be fair
But it's us who got us in this mess
Us who caused all this distress
So although we couldn't apprehend it
It's us who really have to mend it

The Plough

Easy as you go
The Clydesdale pulls the plough
Planting for tomorrow
For days when it shall not be here

Clydesdale are for yesteryear
But head down
Never lose the line
Blinkers of leather

Accept the tether and inclement weather
Pull the plough boy
Instructions heeded
To provide for tomorrow
When you shall not be needed

Easy as you go
The Clydesdale pulls the plough
Planting for tomorrow
For days when it shall not be here

Postal Strike

No letters again today
I think it is so rotten
No letters again today
Have I been forgotten?

Have my friends forsaken me?
Has depression overtaken me?
Nobody is writing
It used to be so exciting

Letterbox rattles first thing
Opening letters the postmen bring
It isn't like that anymore
He doesn't walk up to my door

Has everyone forgotten me?
The end now of my tale
The only people who don't have friends
Are those at Royal Mail

No letters again today
I think it is so rotten
No letters again today
Have I been forgotten?

Fox Hunting Ban

I don't like foxes
Well not very much
They've beautiful eyes
But scary to touch
And yet I love them so much
When I see them run
Escaping a pack of hounds or a gun

Who are we?
To judge who lives on this Earth?
Who are we?
To decide what others are worth?
A fox kills chickens so do we
Perhaps I do like foxes
More than foxes like me

.

The Carbon Footprint

I want the carbon footprint to grow forever smaller
That way my children have a chance to grow forever
taller
I want the carbon footprint to incredibly diminish
And I mean to make a mark and play my part before I
finish

Polar bears struggling on melting ice
Drifting to nowhere is not very nice
I want the carbon footprint to become less and less
I want our politicians to sort out this dreadful mess

I fear that none are listening but I so wish that they can
Be they in the States or England, China or Japan
Politicians never listen, blurred by their own desires
But please sort the carbon footprint before the globe
expires

Time For Change

I'm tired of all MP's
Grey suits
Grey brains
Are there better ones than these?
I'm tired of all the lies
The grey grins
Nobody wins
Can we bring them down to size?
I'm tired of their decisions
We voted for these guys
All we get are packs of lies
I'm tired of all MP's

Carbon Flippers

Carbon emits from the sea
Deposits into the air
The sea is overflowing now
Full to the brim with our wastes
Carbon footprints everywhere
Mending as we tread
Maybe carbon flippers too?
Or the Dead Sea won't be the only sea that's dead

Since The Romans

Ever since the straight-nosed Romans
Straightened all our roads
Straightened all our walls
And straightened all our clothes
We've entered the social circles
We've welcomed strangers in
Regardless of persuasion
Or colour of their skin

And that's the way it should be
It's always been the same
We'd be in a right old state
If the Romans never came
And they were nasty devils
Who loved to rape and pillage
They all drank too much wine

As they passed through every village
So people coming to our country
To start their lives anew
Has been going on for centuries
It's nothing really new
They have changed us for the better
As we adopted their ideas
It's something we should welcome
Because it's been that way for years

If You Were The Only Girl

If you were the only girl in the World
And I was the only boy
We could go in a pub without being afraid
We could go in a club without being on parade

We could get a Chinese without having to wait
We could even get married without a debate
If you were the only girl in the World
And I was the only boy

We'd be the only pair on the beach
We'd learn to jet ski no-one else there to teach
We'd dance until the dawn of next day
Leave a restaurant without paying

There'd be no-one to pay
Get on a flight no queue once again
But hang on, which one of us
Will try to fly the damn plane?

Printed in Great Britain
by Amazon